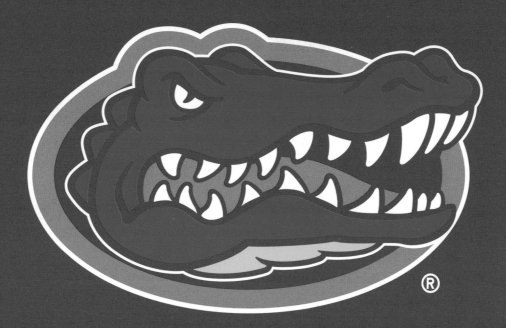

®

To my friends and colleagues at Forest High School in Ocala, Florida who have provided much encouragement, great insight, and very helpful critiques for all of my Gator books and other Gator Goodies. We are the "Forest Family. ~ Mark "Dr. D" Damohn

For Donna-You have made my walk through this life a wonderful, love-filled journey. ~ Tim Williams

Teach a child how to enjoy reading and you will empower his soul to soar, his mind to stretch and his creativity to fruition. ~ Michele Leilani of michelesphotorestorations.com

Use of the lyrics to "My Favorite Springs" is courtesy of Cynthia L. Johnson, coordinator for The Ichetucknee Partnership, Lake City, FL.

Best Wishes
Mark "Dr D" Damohn
Go Gators !!!.

ISBN 13: 978-1-936319-56-5
ISBN 10: 1-936319-56-X

PRT0711A

Printed in the United States.

GO GATORS!

# Albert and Alberta's

## Great

# FLORIDA

### Road Trip

Written by Mark "Dr. D" Damohn    Illustrated by Tim Williams

School is out.
It's vacation for the summer.
Albert says "If we stay home and pout
Then that would be a bummer."


Alberta, always cheerful and bright,
Says, "Let's go on a Florida road trip."
Albert jumps up and says, "That sounds right."
"Let's load it up and let it rip."

"Where should we go? What should we do?"
"Why don't we visit our own home state?"
"Let's round up the family and the whole crew."
"For there is no state greater for us Florida Gators."

Along with family and friends
They load up the ole' van Bug.
Where will they go? Well, it depends !!
But they are as snug as a bug in a rug.


So on the road they go.
Where they will wind up
We really don't know.
But will they make new friends? YUP !!


But that is what is so great
About an unplanned vacation.
Go here. Go there
Without a planned destination.

There are some cousins who live in Palatka.
They are known for their great Florida stew.
And they are native-born Florida Crackers.
What the stew is made of nobody has a clue.


Now, Albert sure is a hungry Gator,
And you know he loves his food.
Eat a little now; eat a little bit later
"Florida stew always puts me in a good mood!"

So after chomping down a nice dinner
And a cruise on the Saint Johns,
Albert thinks, "This is a winner."
"What great scenery, and what lovely ponds."


Cruising on a boat and tasting some big eats
Sure is a nice way to start this summer vacation.
It's time to slumber and dream of sweet treats.
With family and friends and Florida relaxation.

Now it is time to say goodbye.
It's off to Jacksonville
And Albert is going to fly.
You know this is going to be a really big thrill.

Albert is special and a pilot's wings he earned.
So over the river and around the trees,
He banked and turned.
Albert flies with the greatest of ease.

Albert is a very good aviator
Which means he's good with flaps.
Alberta says, "Not too bad for a Gator!"
Albert could put it on auto and take an aerial nap.

Since Albert's such a skilled flyer
He sets down at the Jacksonville Landing
Alberta is impressed and really does admire.
"Learning how to fly must sure be demanding!"

Albert and Alberta go to the beaches of Jax.
They go surfing and swimming
To run, play and to simply relax.
The fun is very much brimming.
Now it is time for a snack.


With beach shovel and bucket
He looks for his favorite food,
Corn-Dog Nuggets.
It's for these yummies that he is in the mood.

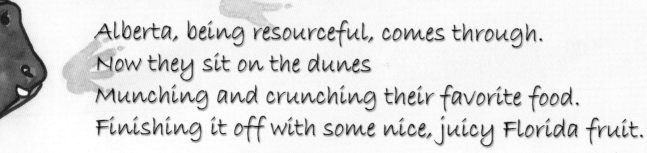

Alberta, being resourceful, comes through.
Now they sit on the dunes
Munching and crunching their favorite food.
Finishing it off with some nice, juicy Florida fruit.

They're on the First Coast
Their vacation is going great.
They are in St. Augustine, which is the most.
Albert and Alberta are at the city's Gate.

Then to the San Marcos castle.
Albert and Alberta are climbing the walls.
They are on vacation. There's no hassle.
Let's hope they don't fall.

Back in the van down A-1-A
Daytona Beach is only miles away.
Even the Boardwalk is a great place to play.
Albert and Alberta have something else planned today.

They go over to the Daytona Speedway.
Albert is going to put on a driving display.
He is in a NASCAR race today.
His driving is more than OK.

Now they are heading down I-95
Jamming to the music while they juke and jive.
But -- uh oh! They take a wrong turn.
And end up on International Drive.


But it's a Florida road trip, so it's OK
They know where they are.
Albert and Alberta are in a land that is so cachet.
Close to the homes of Hollywood movie stars.

They are in the city of Orlando
It's vacation and dress is casual
Albert is visiting his cousin, Fernando.
Check out Albert, wearing his sandals!

They are at their cousin's house,
Near the land of seals and whales.
Fernando, along with his spouse,
Says, "We'll have so much fun here, it never fails."

There are magical castles in the air
In the land of a friendly old Mouse.
Where the weather is always fair.
Albert and Alberta are ready to rouse.

So after some sharing and a nice little nap
They are all set to go and keep to their plan.
Albert is ready to roll and puts on his cap.
They can't wait to see the family at Gatorland.


Albert, being the good guest
Shows up with some of his favorite fried chicken
So Albert feeds his cousins fast.
For the pace of their vacation now quickens.

Albert and Alberta are on the Beeline
Going directly east to that special place.
Going to the Cape it's so mighty fine.
They want to meet America's heroes of Outer Space.

Albert and Alberta proceed on their way.
Palm Bay-- Like so many Florida towns
Albert and Alberta like Palm Bay.
With senior citizens here, the town really resounds.

Albert and Alberta agree with that.
Florida is the place where the good life is at.
Sun, surf, golf, Panama Hats
Shuffleboard, pink flamingos, and all that!

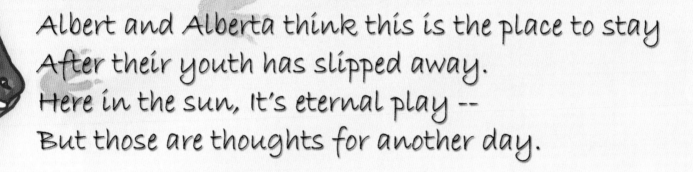

Albert and Alberta think this is the place to stay
After their youth has slipped away.
Here in the sun, It's eternal play --
But those are thoughts for another day.

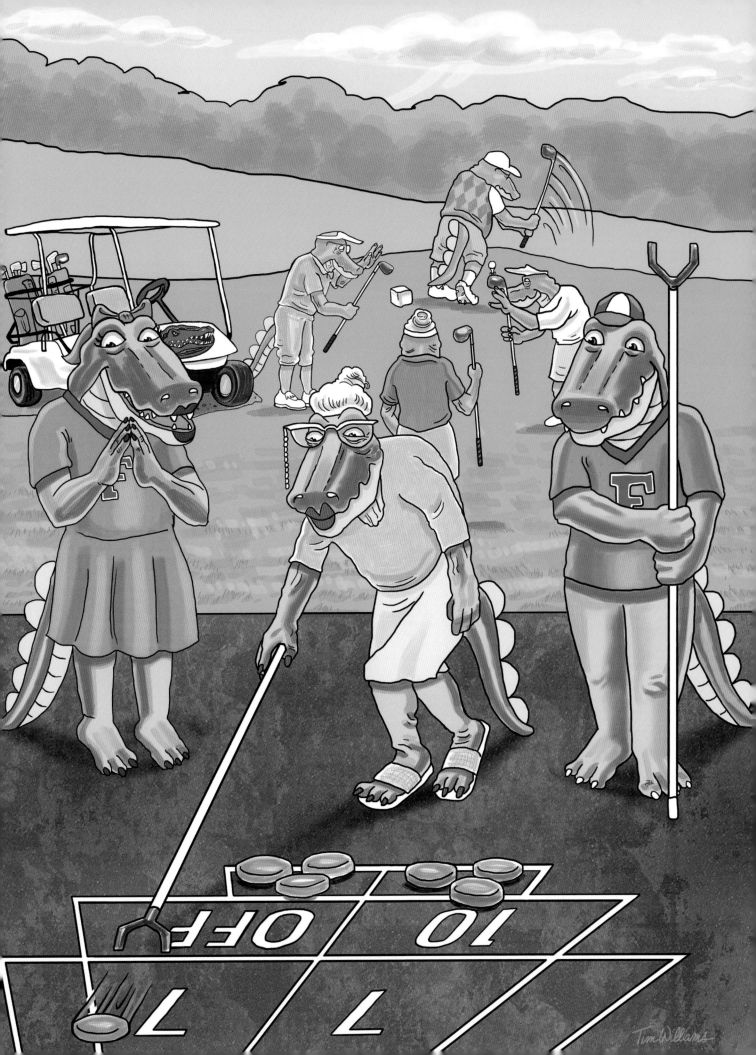

Now Albert and Alberta are in Miami
Albert loves performing down in South Beach
He's such a great rapper he'll win a Grammy,
He's ready to growl. He's ready to screech.

There is no rap star who can meet his beats.
Tapping their feet, these Gator heads are bobbin'.
Albert stands alone out in the street.
The base is low and loud, the Gators are throbbin'.

So after Miami it's off to the Keys they go.
What will they find?
We just don't know.
But fun is definitely on their mind.


Albert and Alberta are in Marathon.
Looking at the tropical fish among the coral reefs
It is time to get their scuba gear on.
Away from the heat. What a relief.

They come across an old Spanish shipwreck.
Albert gets gold in his eyes.
"Let's give it a check."
Albert finds some gold doubloons
Much to his surprise.

Later Albert is feeling pretty sporty
Albert does a Jimmy Buffett reprise.
He does his best "A Pirate Looks at 40"
And Alberta rolls her eyes and just sighs.

Visions of swashbuckling are a flash
In his Errol Flynn's pirate mind.
With all these tales of golden cash
Albert should have been born in another time.

Back to the present day, back to Key Largo
Albert and Alberta along with family and friends
Get a charter boat so they can all go
Fishing for the tasty tuna of the Blue Fin.

Deep sea fishing is such a good sport.
The water is choppy, Alberta casts her line.
They are far at sea, miles away from port.
She lands a sailfish in absolutely no time.

They are leaving the Keys, heading to the Glades
And they are driving across Alligator Alley
To see how real alligators have it made.
They're going to meet Alberta's cousin Sally.


Sally has a special treat in mind
They are going to ride in an air boat.
For Albert and Alberta are one of her kind.
Albert is scared and hopes it can float.

Albert and Alberta are met with arms open wide.
Albert and Alberta are big-time stars.
For they are famous down Everglade side.
Since they're mascots of the best university by far.


Albert and Alberta show them how to do
The world famous Gator Chomp.
While their cousins show them how to
Romp and stomp in the real Swamp.

A good time is had by all.
The sun is starting to set low.
All are having fun and having a ball.
So Albert and Alberta don't want to go.

Something has been set off in their reptilian brains.
Unwisely, Albert hangs around to see,
Off to the southeast is the start of a hurricane.
Something he really ought to flee.

The wind starts to blow
And the rain starts to pelt.
The storm starts to grow.
He thinks he might melt !!!

Albert wished that out of there he could fly.
Albert is so shaken with fear
It really is time to say goodbye.
He thinks his time might be near.

But, by morning the wind subsides
And the rains subdue.
Albert thinks if he stays outside
He might catch the flu.


They are back in their van on Alligator Alley.
Albert was shaken by his close call
But his spirit soon rallies
Because he is safe with his ma and pa.

Ever since Albert was a very little tot
He liked to collect seashells.
He liked to collect them a lot.
The sea breeze he started to smell.

But Albert has never been to the isle of Sanibel.
For Albert this will be a great surprise.
All Gators know this place is really swell.
In the land under the Florida deep-blue skies.

Nothing but shells from dunes to the sea.
"This place must be shell heaven,"
Albert says, not hiding his glee,
"Let stay from seven to eleven."

Everyone wanted to see the Greatest Show on Earth
So many animals, high wire, and clowns
All were filled with great mirth.
All the great sights, smells, and sounds.

Back on the interstate and headed to Tampa Bay.
Albert and Alberta are in for a sweet treat.
For they're going to ride the roller coaster throughout the day.
For a couple of Gators, that's a pretty neat seat!

Albert and Alberta are visiting their friend Manny the Manatee.
They are going to meet at the amusement park
So they notify Manny with an email tweet.
Albert and Alberta love taking rides from dawn to dark.

Now on I-4 and heading east to the county of Polk
They are on their way to see some more of their folks.
All are having such a great time as onward they drove
Passing miles and miles of citrus groves.

Albert and Alberta love to farm
Being out in nature has such a strong charm.
Both love to plow and till the Florida fresh soil.
And there all their horses and cattle they love to spoil.

Albert loves to fish, so he gets his wish.
For Florida large mouth Bass make such a tasty dish.
So off to Lake County which is the land of lakes.
Albert and his friend Larry in a fishing tournament they partake.

Larry's wife Diane does not like to fish.
Being in the boat is not her wish.
She and Alberta on the shore they sat.
Talking about this. Talking about that.

They come to Ocala to see their Gator buds.
Alberta loves each and every one of her horses.
All the colts, mares, and studs.
She loves to watch them race around the courses.


Ocala thoroughbreds have hooves that are fleet.
Albert thinks, "If my Gators could run this sweet.
All of our foes would know nothing but defeat"
For this is the ultimate track meet.


Now, off to see the wonderful springs.
They feel like Mother Nature's Queens and Kings
Albert and Alberta will see such wonderful things.
Where their hearts open up and they sing.

*sung to the tune of My Favorite Things

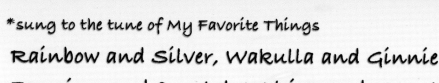

Rainbow and Silver, Wakulla and Ginnie
Fanning and Crystal, Wekiva and Manatee
Memories of outings, what joy they all bring
These are a few of our favorite springs.

Herons and gators and turtles and otters
All make their home in the crystal-blue waters.
Crayfish and catfish and birds on the wing.
All can be viewed at our natural springs!

Homosassa, Ichetucknee, Mother Nature's bling
For swimming and diving and tubing and things,
You've just gotta love our springs!!

They are on the Gulf at Cedar Key
"Seafood galore, as much as you please!
Now this is the Gator life for you and me!"
As the sun sets into the shining sea.

Now after a time with great Gator friends
It's on the road all over again
For new adventures to begin.
They make a special stop at A.F.B. Eglin.


The Air Force has been waiting for Albert
For they know he is a pilot.
Everybody knows he's an expert,
And they are going to let him fly it.

Albert is flying a state-of-the art F-22
Heading over the Florida Gulf Coast
Albert knows this is something that he can boast.
He feels pretty keen
In that flying machine.


Over Pensacola, which is a Navy town.
He flies around Fort Picks
In that new F-22 low and down.
He show them some flying Gator tricks.

Back to the base since he is running out of gas
Albert gently sets the plane down.
So he can meet all  the brass.
They've all come down
And are glad he's in town.

As Albert and Alberta start to head back home
There is a place they have to go to and they can't wait
It's a place that, to them, is so well known.
Why, it's the capital of our great state.

Albert and Alberta are going to Tally
Which you know is the Land of the 'Noles
Albert feels uneasy,
But still he goes.

From Lake City, down I-75
While it has been a great trip.
But it also has been a long drive.
Heading back home now, they start to zip.

It has been a great summer vacation
Spending time with family and friends.
They talk about their favorite locations
They discovered before their road trip ends.

Back to Gainesville and back to what they know.
The dorms, the Swamp, and the O'Dome.
May it ever be so humble, and these Gators they go--
There is no place they'd rather be than home, sweet home!